Dinner at Five

A True Story

by Ruth I. Peterson   *illustrations by* Nathan Y. Jarvis

OWL'S HOUSE PRESS
LOS ALTOS, CALIFORNIA

Dinner at Five

ISBN: 1-891992-00-7
Library of Congress Number: 98-065646

First Edition
10 9 8 7 6 5 4 3 2 1

To order:
OWL'S HOUSE PRESS
4966 El Camino Real, Suite #118
Los Altos, CA 94022
1-888-848-OWLS

WWW.OWLSHOUSE.COM

To little girls with big ideas and big hearts to match.

One Sunday afternoon Ruthie decided to have a party.

But she didn't tell her mother.

Ruthie had gone to the kitchen and watched Grandmother make an angelfood cake. Egg whites from a dozen eggs stood up in a stiff peak. Grandmother's cheeks puffed in and out as she whistled and added sugar and flour to the mound of egg whites.

Good smells were coming from Grandmother's pies that were cooling on the window sill and from the loaves of bread mother had just taken from the oven.

Chicken was frying on the stove. Daddy was making peach ice cream and turning the handle of the freezer as he poured more salt on the ice. Mother turned the chicken and looked at Daddy.

"It will be good to have family here today. Aunt Irene is coming and bringing Hazel and Gladys."

Daddy kept turning the handle. "Mother," he said, "I forgot to tell you. Uncle Charlie and Aunt Ruth are coming today, too."

"That's all right," said Mother. She looked around her at the pies and cake and bread and chicken. "There's plenty to eat—enough for the entire town!"

Ruthie pictured all the people in Dudley, Illinois, coming to her house for dinner.

"Wouldn't that be fun?" she thought. "If I invite the whole town to dinner, Mother will be so pleased! We can have a party! That's what I'll do. I'll invite everyone in Dudley." But she didn't tell her mother.

Ruthie went to her room and put on her new taffeta dress that made happy, crinkly noises and went out into the street. She walked from door to door saying over and over, "Come to my house for dinner. We eat at five."

Miss Lucy, Miss Mary, and Miss Jenny, the three old ladies who lived in the house on the corner, asked if they could call Ruthie's mother to thank her.

"Our phone doesn't work," Ruthie said.

When Mrs. Baker heard the invitation, she questioned Ruthie, "Am I supposed to bring the children?"

"Oh, yes," said Ruthie, "My mother loves children."

"But no one ever invites *six* children," said Mrs. Baker.

"Mother does," said Ruthie, "Bring the dog, too. Mother loves dogs." She patted the greyhound's head.

When she had knocked on every door in town, Ruthie went home.
"Where have you been?" asked Mother.
"Visiting," said Ruthie.
But she didn't tell her mother about the party.

At five o'clock the doorbell rang.
"It's the folks," said Mother. "Answer the door, Bill."
Daddy looked up from the freezer. "I'm packing the ice cream."
So Mother went.

Mother opened the door. There were Mr. and Mrs. Baker and Susan, and Gregory, and Alice, and Chris, and Tony, and Travis, and the dog. Mother looked puzzled.

"Nice of you to send Ruthie to ask us for dinner," said Mrs. Baker.

Mother gasped. "Come in," she managed to say.

Ruthie beamed. "Wait till the rest of Dudley gets here," she thought. "Then Mother will smile." Ruthie patted the greyhound.

Mother told Ruthie to get Daddy as the doorbell rang again. When Mother opened the door, she saw people on the porch, on the sidewalk, and on the street.

"What a great idea, Mrs. Thompson... having us all to dinner," said the postmaster.

Daddy and Ruthie came to stand by her as Mother opened the door wider and motioned for the guests to come in. Her face turned pink.

"Isn't she pretty?" thought Ruthie. "I knew she'd be pleased."

"How nice of you to come," said Mother. Daddy shook hands with everyone as they came in. His face was purplish, and his left hand was clenched.

"Daddy's face looks strange. Maybe he's sick," thought Ruthie. "I hope he won't miss the party." Daddy put his arm around Mother to steady her.

The living room was full. The dining room was full. There were people in the hall. Ninety-nine people had arrived. Mother stopped counting when the doorbell rang.

It was the relatives. Aunt Irene, Hazel, Gladys, Uncle Charlie, and Aunt Ruth stared at the crowd of people.

"Didn't know you were having a party," said Uncle Charlie.

"It was my surprise," said Ruthie. She smiled at her mother.

Mother didn't smile back.

Mother's face got redder and redder as she and Daddy ran back and forth from the cellar and the storeroom bringing cans and cans of home-canned fruits and vegetables and home-cured hams.

Ruthie never had seen her mother look as pretty as at her party.

But Mother didn't smile.

When Daddy made tables out on the lawn with saw horses and boards, Grandmother covered them with tablecloths. Everyone helped bring out the ham that Daddy sliced and fresh bread and ice cream and chicken and vegetables and fruits and cake and pies and cookies from the cookie jar. Jenny Young went back to the house on the corner for more silverware.

As everyone laughed and ate, Mrs. Bottomley exclaimed, "Mrs. Thompson, you are fabulous. Who would have thought to invite the entire town? You must like every one of us."

"I do indeed," said Mother. She looked at the happy faces around her and began to smile as everyone praised her good food. Ruthie beamed.

"I knew she'd be happy," thought Ruthie.

Later, Ruthie stood by the door with Mother and Daddy as the guests left to go home. She said good-bye to all her friends as they thanked her and her mother and father.

Ruthie decided when she grew up that she would give lots and lots of parties.

Mother slumped in a chair. Daddy sat down, too, and put his hands under his legs to keep from using them on Ruthie. Instead, he told her to go to bed. She looked at Mother.

"Wasn't our party wonderful?"

Mother crossed her fingers. "Wonderful," she sighed.

Ruthie smiled and went to bed.

Grandmother shook her head. She looked at Mother. "Why didn't you talk to Ruthie?" she asked in a disgusted tone.

Mother sighed, "I was too tired!"

Upstairs Ruthie was in bed, smoothing the top sheet with her hands and thinking how she would make Daddy happy.